Seren Kitty

Seren's Aunt Tilda is a witch, but not a very good one. When she accidentally turns Seren into a cat, it causes mayhem. But can it help Seren beat the school bully?

COPYRIGHT

Published by 3AD Publishing

Also by Mandy Martin:
Seren Kitty: and the Tricky Wizard
Seren Kitty and the Dog-Nappers
Seren Kitty in Italy
Moon Pony
Will on the Water

Chapter One

"Mum! Can I go and see Aunt Tilda after school?"

Seren rushed into the kitchen, her black hair flying behind her like a crow's wing. Mum was making cakes for the bake sale.

"I have to dress up as a cat for school tomorrow," Seren added. "I thought Tilda could help me with my costume."

Aunt Tilda was great at making things, especially because she cheated and used magic. Even if it did go a little bit wrong now and then.

"Do you think that's a good idea?" Mum said, brushing flour from her hands. "Last time Aunt Tilda helped you with a school project, she dyed your hair green."

Mum sighed. "It's lucky it was the end of term

or Mrs Spigglebottom would have been furious."

Mrs Spigglebottom was Seren's headmistress. Luckily, she didn't know that Seren's Aunt could do magic.

"Besides," Mum added, "I can help you with your costume."

"That's all right, Mum," Seren said quickly, "You're busy enough with the baking."

Seren loved her mum, but she wasn't very good at craft. Her cakes were delicious though.

"Can I go? To Aunt Tilda's after school?" Seren tilted her head and gave a huge toothy grin.

"I suppose so," Mum said. "Just make sure she doesn't try to do anything *special*."

By special Mum meant magical.

"Okay," Seren said, grabbing her bag and running for the bus, "I promise."

"What costume are you wearing tomorrow?" Seren's best friend Freia asked as Seren sat next to her on the bus. "I can't decide whether to be something easy like Alice from *Alice in Wonderland*, or be like everyone else and come as Hermione Granger."

"Alice would be easy," Seren agreed. Freia had long straight blonde hair. "You'd just need a blue dress and an apron."

"Megan did that last year, though." Freia said with a frown. Megan was her big sister.

Seren smiled in sympathy. She would never want to wear the same as her big brother Bryn. No chance of that. He was going as Harry Potter. His whole class were.

"What about you?" Freia asked. "What character are you going to be?"

"I thought I'd go as a cat. Maybe the one from *The Owl and the Pussycat*."

"You and cats!" Freia laughed.

Seren blushed. "It's just that I can't have a cat, what with Dad being allergic. So dressing up as one is the next best thing."

"Didn't you go as a cat last year?"

Seren grimaced and nodded. "Wilbur from *Winnie the Witch*. But I looked more like the witch than the cat, with my bogey-green hair."

Freia giggled. "It suited you. It made a change from black *and* it matched your eyes."

Seren leaned in closer and made sure no one was listening. "It was Aunt Tilda's fault. I'm going over tonight, but Mum says, 'don't let her do anything *special*'."

Freia gave an understanding nod. She was the only person outside Seren's family who knew about her magical aunt.

"I'm sure it will be fine," Freia said. "Just don't ask for whiskers!"

Chapter Two

Seren felt like the end of the day would never come.

She'd forgotten her French homework in her rush for the bus and Madame Cheval had made her sit by herself as punishment.

Then it had been meatballs for lunch. Seren loved meatballs. Unfortunately she never got to eat them because, every time they were on the menu, Billy made a point of knocking her plate into her lap.

"You have to tell a teacher," Freia said, as she helped Seren change into a spare skirt from lost property.

"What's the point? They'll say something at circle time about how bullying is wrong, and he'll just smirk and push me over next chance he gets."

Billy was the only part of school that Seren hated. It didn't matter how much she stayed out of his way, or how often she tried to *rise above it*, as Bryn told her to, Billy found some way to make her cry.

"It's not just you he picks on," Freia said. "He locked Nadeem in a toilet last week. And poor Misaki ran out of Music because he said her recorder playing sounded like a goose with a sore throat."

"Well, maybe he won't recognise me in my cat costume tomorrow," Seren said hopefully. "At least then I'll get one day of peace."

At last it was home time. Seren waved as Freia got on the bus without her, and then she walked the short distance to her Aunt Tilda's house.

"Aunt Tilda? Are you home?" Seren called, as she used the spare key under the concrete frog to let herself in.

"In the study!" a cheerful voice called.

Seren said hello to Fizz and Bang, Tilda's cats, before making her way to the back of the house. Aunt Tilda's study was really the dining room. But she had filled it with amazing things like spell books and jars of magic ingredients. There was even a cauldron, although Tilda said she preferred to use the gas hob.

"Hello, poppet," Tilda said, as Seren poked her head around the door. Her aunt's bright red hair was a mess of tangled curls, with two pencils and a wand making a bun at the back. She jangled with bangles and necklaces and her long skirts snagged on the furniture as she came forward to give Seren a hug.

"Hi, Aunt Tilda," Seren said, "Is it safe to come in?"

The room glittered with silver smoke and smelled of beetroot and daffodils.

"Of course! Don't mind this." Tilda waved her hand, making the smoke swirl and spiral like fog.

"Just a little experiment. Have you come to learn some magic?"

"Not today." Seren shook her head in emphasis. Mum would not be happy if she knew Aunt Tilda was trying to teach her some spells. As far as Mum was concerned, Tilda was the only *special* person in the family. She didn't know that Seren had what Tilda called *talent*.

"I need a cat costume for school, and you know how Mum is at craft."

Tilda looked disappointed. Then she brightened up. "You'll need some ears and whiskers then? I can do that." She rummaged through a pile of books that threatened to topple to the floor.

"Wait, I know it's here somewhere. Where is it?" She pulled a large book with a purple velvet cover from the bottom of the heap and dumped it on the table. Flicking through the pages, she eventually said, "Ah ha!" and smiled at Seren.

"This is it. How to turn someone into a cat."

"No, Aunt Tilda!" Seren squealed. "I don't want to *be* a cat. I just need a costume, with ears and a tail. Like the one we did last year."

"Oh yes, the green hair. That was my favourite. I could do it white this year for a change?"

"A white costume, yes that would be great. But no magic. I promised Mum."

Tilda sighed. "Spoil sport." She slammed the book shut and her bottom lip jutted out, just like Bryn's did when Mum and Dad told him off.

"I could ask Mum to help me if you'd rather?"

"No, it's fine," Tilda said. "Your mum was always the sensible one, even when we were little. *Bor*-ing."

Seren laughed and took her aunt's hand. "Come on," she said, "let's find your sewing machine. It'll be fun."

Chapter Three

Several hours later, Tilda and Seren had managed to turn a white bedsheet into a passable cat costume, complete with hood and ears.

"We just need to add the tail," Seren said as she tried it on. "Then I'll get Mum to draw some whiskers on my cheeks and Billy will never know it's me."

"Is that boy still bothering you?" Tilda asked in concern. "I can teach you some protective spells if you like."

Seren shook her head. Tilda's spells always went wonky. Billy was enough trouble without any help from Tilda.

"It's fine," Seren said. "It's nearly the end of term and hopefully he won't be in my class next year." That didn't explain how she would avoid him at break times, but she had the whole summer holidays to worry about that.

Seren pinned on the tail and gave a twirl. "How do I look?"

Tilda clapped. "Almost like a real cat. We just need to do this." Her eyes twinkled as she reached into the kitchen drawer and pulled out a wand.

"Tilda Tee, hear me say,

Turn my girl into a cat today!"

"Aunt Tilda, no!" Seren cried.

But it was too late. She felt as if a whole army of ants were marching across her skin. Then she shivered, and goosebumps rose along her arms. Only they weren't goosebumps, they were little white hairs that thickened into fur. She opened her mouth to protest, but all that came out was a yowl. Then the kitchen table started to grow, until it towered above her. No, it hadn't grown. She had shrunk!

Seren looked down and yowled again at the

sight of white paws where her hands used to be. Turning round she caught a glimpse of a long white tail twisting up behind her.

"Tilda, turn me back!" she tried to say. But it came out as, "Miaow, mew mew, meeeoowww!"

Tilda seemed to understand, though, because she squatted down next to Seren and stroked her head. Her jangling bracelets sounded like clashing cymbals.

"Quit fussing, I'll turn you back in a mo. I only wanted you to feel what it was like to be a cat. You know, get into character. My, aren't you a cutie!"

"Miaow!" Seren protested.

"Keep your fur on. Here, let me take a picture first." Aunt Tilda patted her pockets, looking for the phone that Seren's mum and dad had bought her for Christmas. She barely knew how it worked and was always asking Seren for help. After a few attempts she found the camera button and snapped a picture.

Seren peered at the screen. Looking back was

a small white cat with one black ear and a splodge of black on its nose. Its eyes were green like hers, but they were cats' eyes.

"Mew mew miaow!" she said, meaning, "Change me back now!"

Tilda sighed. "Okay." She stood up and fetched her wand.

"Tilda hay, Tilda hen,

Turn the cat into Seren."

Nothing happened.

Tilda tried again. She shook her wand and then rubbed it on her top. The third attempt didn't work either.

Oh no, Seren thought. Mum's going to go loopy. That's if I don't get shooed out the house for making Dad sneeze.

Chapter Four

"Intruder!" a voice yowled in Seren's ear. She spun round, nearly standing on her own tail.

It was Fizz. She was a little black cat with yellow eyes, although she didn't look so tiny now.

"Fizz, it's me, Seren."

"Seren? The small human who visits Matilda?"

"Yes, that's right." Seren sighed with relief. Someone finally understood her.

"Whatever happened? Why are you pretending to be a cat? I do hope you are not intending to steal our dinner."

"You should leave," Bang said, coming to stand behind Fizz. "We do not like strangers." Bang was a large tabby, with one ear ragged and torn. He towered over Seren now like a tiger.

"I'm not a stranger," Seren said urgently. Fizz and Bang didn't look so friendly when they were twice her size. "And I definitely don't want to eat cat food. I just want to be me again."

"I suppose Matilda muddled up one of her spells?" Fizz said wearily.

Seren nodded.

Fizz licked a paw and cleaned her nose. "We would never have come to be witches' cats for her if we had known how bad she was."

"You're witches' cats?" Seren asked in amazement.

"Of course," Bang replied. "We help Matilda with many of her spells."

"Can you help her turn me back into a girl again?"

Fizz and Bang glanced at each other. Bang stretched and arched his back. "We will see what we can do.".

Seren followed Fizz and Bang to Tilda's study. The witch was frantically searching through more books, muttering to herself.

"There must be a counter spell. Or an undo spell, or a *turn my niece back into a girl before my sister finds out s*pell."

"Aunt Tilda!" Seren called, but Fizz and Bang shook their heads.

"Leave this to us," Fizz said. She jumped on the table and walked backwards and forwards. Seren had seen her do it a hundred times before.

"Go away, pesky cat," Tilda said. "I don't have time to pet you now."

"Doesn't Aunt Tilda know you're trying to help?" Seren asked Bang.

He shook his head. "I am afraid your Aunt does not speak very good Cat. We try to teach her, but she thinks we are asking for food." He looked up as Fizz pushed some books aside and then started to wash herself.

"Get down, Fizz," Tilda said. Then she cried, "There it is! I knew I'd find it. That's the book I need."

Fizz jumped down and joined Seren and Bang.

"Don't you mind that she doesn't know you're helping?" Seren asked.

Fizz shrugged. "What does it matter as long as we help? That is our purpose."

"Seren, jump up here, there's a good girl. I mean cat." Tilda patted a chair covered in shawls and cushions. It looked a long way up.

"I can't jump up there! It's as high as a house."

"Nonsense," Fizz said. "You merely crouch and jump, there is nothing to it."

Seren wasn't sure, but she couldn't see any way to climb up and Tilda was busy with her spell book. She crouched low, feeling the spring building in her legs. Then she jumped as hard as she could.

It felt like flying.

Instead of landing on the seat of the chair she landed high on the back. It was narrow and she wobbled, her tail waving around behind her as she tried to find her balance.

Carefully Seren jumped down onto the seat.

"Wow!" she called down to Fizz and Bang. "That was amazing! It's like being on a trampoline."

Just then, Tilda came over and read carefully from a spell book.

"*Hay-dee hee, lay-dee lee,*

Magic come and work for me.

Undo the spell that I have done,

Bring an end to all this fun."

She flourished her wand and Seren waited.

Slowly Seren felt the same sensations as before, but in reverse. Her skin stretched like an overfilled balloon and her arms and legs itched as if she had nits. After a moment she was sitting on the chair, wearing the cat costume.

Fizz and Bang both gave a satisfied, "Miaow," before swaying sinuously from the room.

"It worked!" Seren said. "Thanks Fizz, thanks Bang."

"Why are you thanking the cats?" Tilda asked, looking a little put out. "It was my spell."

Seren felt guilty. Was it a secret that they were

witches' cats? She wasn't sure. "They kept me company," she said to Tilda, "that's all."

Chapter Five

"She really changed you into a cat?" Freia's eyes were wide as Seren told her all about it on the bus the following morning.

"Uh huh," Seren nodded. "It was freaky. The world was huge, and my skin itched, and the only creatures who could understand me were Fizz and Bang, Aunt Tilda's cats."

"But she changed you back okay? No lasting effects?" Freia looked her up and down, as if checking for green hair or whiskers.

"None that I can see," Seren said. "Thankfully. Can you imagine Mrs Spigglebottom's face if I turned into a cat in assembly?" She shivered. It was a horrible thought.

"Well, your costume is great," Freia added.

"Yours too," Seren said. Freia had come as the singing mermaid. Her mum was very good at making costumes. Her tail shimmered every time she moved.

"Hey, Seren," a voice called as they got off the bus. "What are you, a zombie? Or did you just have a fight with your mum's sheets?"

"Shut up, Billy," Freia snapped, putting her arm through Seren's. "At least Seren made an effort and didn't just put on a shop bought thing."

"Don't, Freia. If you answer back it makes him worse. Let's go."

Freia nodded and the girls hurried into the classroom, sitting as close to the teacher as they could.

They had Literacy first. It was Seren's favourite lesson. Making up stories wasn't difficult when you had a crazy aunt like Tilda. Every day with her was an adventure.

She soon forgot all about Billy's taunts as she concentrated on the task. They had to write a story about being an animal.

Well, that's easy-peasy, Seren thought. I don't have to imagine, I just have to remember.

She bent close to the paper and thought about the night before and what it had felt like to be small and furry.

Suddenly she sensed someone watching her. Turning her head slightly she saw Miss Joy reading her work.

"That's a very imaginative story, Seren," she said. "May I read it to the class?"

Seren nodded happily.

After Miss Joy had finished reading the story, the class clapped. But as they went out for morning break, Billy came up behind Seren and sniggered.

"Hey, cat girl! Got fleas?" He pushed past and began chanting, "Seren's got fleas, Seren's got fleas."

"Ignore him," Freia whispered. "Come on, let's go to the small playground."

But Billy followed them through, teasing Seren

like a cat tormenting a mouse.

"Oh, leave off, Billy, no one thinks it's funny," Freia said crossly. But they did. Billy's usual gang of supporters were all laughing and pointing at Seren.

Seren could feel her face getting hot and she couldn't wait for break to be over. The more Billy chanted, the angrier she got.

And then something awful happened. A terribly familiar feeling crept over her skin, a feeling like marching ants.

"Seren," Freia hissed, "Are you okay? You've gone white and … and furry!"

Seren ducked her head and ran for the girls' toilets. She hurtled into a cubicle and slammed the door. Just in time. The change completed and she was suddenly on the floor staring up at the toilet above her.

She crouched and leapt, like Fizz and Bang had taught her, and jumped onto the windowsill. What was she going to do?

"Seren, are you in here?" It was Freia. Seren

28

miaowed quietly.

"Oh no!" Freia said softly. "Have you turned into a cat again? Do you want me to go and find a teacher?"

Seren jumped to the floor and crawled under the door. She shook her head at Freia. The last thing she needed was a teacher calling her mum.

Seren took a deep breath. Think, Seren, think. As she calmed down her skin prickled. She felt her body stretch like a water balloon and suddenly she was herself again, just as the bell rang for class.

"Phew!" she said to Freia. "That was close."

Chapter Six

The rest of the day crept by slower than a lame snail. Seren watched the clock but the hands stubbornly refused to move.

I need to see Aunt Tilda, she thought over and over. She has to fix this. Now!

Billy kept up his taunting all through Numeracy and Music, but it was PE that Seren dreaded most. What if she started to change in front of everybody?

"May I have your attention, class," Miss Joy said, clapping her hands.

Seren looked up guiltily. Had she been caught daydreaming?

"In place of PE this afternoon we have a special treat for you all."

Seren grinned in relief. No PE!

"As it is National Children's Fiction Day, we will be hearing from a special visitor – local author Ivor Storey."

For the first time since morning break, Seren smiled. She wasn't likely to get cross listening to an author – she loved stories and hearing about how they were written.

The class walked in single file to the hall behind Miss Joy. Seren tried to sit next to Freia, but Miss Joy called out, "Stay in line, children."

"Too bad," a voice whispered behind her. "Looks like you're stuck with me."

It was Billy. Seren bit her lip so hard it hurt. Please don't let me change into a cat in the hall, she begged.

She wondered whether to tell Miss Joy she felt poorly. It wasn't a lie, her tummy felt like tangled spaghetti. But she wanted to listen to Ivor Storey. What could Billy do in front of all the teachers anyway?

Seren soon found out. During the whole of the author's talk, all Seren could hear was Billy murmuring, "Seren has fleas, itchy scratchy fleas," again and again until she itched all over. She started to fidget as she felt the imaginary fleas crawling through her hair and hopping in her clothes.

"Seren Adessi, please sit still," Mrs Spigglebottom hissed in a whisper that carried across the hall. All the children turned, craning their necks like meerkats to get a better look. Seren never got told off in assembly.

Seren felt her face redden and she ducked her head, trying to disappear inside her cat costume. But it was too late. The marching ants stomped up her legs and goosebumps rose on her arms.

"Miss, I'm going to be sick!" she said, and ran from the room.

By the time she reached the hall door it looked twice its usual size and she wasn't sure she would be able to push it open. Thankfully it had been left ajar and Seren managed to squeeze through. She landed on all fours and scampered up the corridor.

Where could she go? She wouldn't be able to open the bathroom door as a cat.

Help, she mewed quietly. What am I going to do?

Chapter Seven

Seren heard footsteps and looked around desperately for a place to hide. She was near the coat rack for Year 6. But it was summer term and there were no coats to duck beneath. But there, at the end, was the lost property box, full of misplaced cardigans and bits of PE kit.

Seren dived into the box and buried herself beneath a smelly t-shirt, wrinkling her nose at the pong.

The footsteps passed and then returned a few moments later.

"Seren?" a voice called. It was Miss Joy.

I'm in here, Seren thought. Please go away so I can try and turn myself back.

Luck was on her side, as Miss Joy let herself

back into the hall and the corridor fell silent.

Seren concentrated on being calm. She tried to forget all the mean things Billy had been saying, and that he'd got her into trouble with Mrs Spigglebottom. The problem was, the more she thought about it, the angrier she became.

This is hopeless, she thought. She curled in a tight ball in the corner of the box and mewed sadly. What is Mum going to say?

Mum! Seren smiled. She wouldn't be cross. She would give me a big cuddle and tell me to be brave.

Seren thought about her mum and felt the anger fizz out like a spent firework. What was it Mum told her to do when she was angry? Not count to ten, that was boring. Oh yes, think of a silly joke.

What was the silliest joke she could think of?

Where do wasps go when they're sick? Waspital!

She and Bryn had loved that joke when they

were little and it still made her smile.

Suddenly Seren felt herself stretch – she had to get out of the box! With a miaow and a springing leap she jumped out just as her paws turned back into feet and hands. She slumped against the wall, exhausted.

The school children were still in the hall, listening to the author. Seren dashed to the girls' toilets and splashed water on her face to make it look like she had been sick. Then she crept back to the hall and stood outside the door. Her knees felt wobbly and the knotted pasta was back in her tummy. Would Mrs Spigglebottom tell her off again?

She smiled in relief when Miss Joy saw her through the door and came over.

"Seren! Where were you? Are you all right?"

"Sorry, Miss Joy," Seren said. "I went to the boys' toilets because they were closer." A boy nearby sniggered and she suddenly realised what she'd said.

Don't let Billy hear I was in the boys' toilets, she thought fervently.

"Okay, Seren. Do you still feel sick? Shall I call your parents?"

Seren shook her head. "It's nearly home time. I'll be fine. Honestly!" she added, when Miss Joy looked uncertain.

"Can I sit at the back, though?" she added, "Just in case?" Then she wouldn't have to go back near Billy.

"Of course, sit here by me." Miss Joy pointed to the floor near her chair and Seren sat down gratefully. But she didn't hear a word of the talk. She was too busy wondering how Aunt Tilda was going to fix the spell.

And how she could stay away from Billy until the end of term.

Chapter Eight

"I'm off to Aunt Tilda's house," Seren said as she came into the house from the school bus.

Mum looked at her sternly. "No you're not. Not two nights in a row. Besides, it's bath night."

"Mum! I'm too old for bath night! I'll have a shower at Tilda's."

"You'll do as you're told, young lady. Now upstairs and do your homework while I make tea."

Seren glared at her mum. It wasn't like she was asking to go out with her friends or to the park.

Mum stood with her hands on her hips and tilted her head as if to say, Don't even think about arguing.

Seren sighed loudly and stomped upstairs. It

was so unfair! She flung her bag on her bed and pulled off her cat costume.

I need to see Tilda now!

As the anger built inside her, Seren felt the crawling sensation she was coming to dread.

Not here! Seren looked around urgently, but it was too late. Her room was suddenly huge and she was down among the dirty clothes and scattered books.

What a mess! Seren thought. I must tidy up. Then her cat ears picked up the sound of Mum answering the phone, followed by clomping footsteps. Oh no. She was coming upstairs.

Seren's heart hammered loudly and she searched for somewhere to hide. But if she hid, her mum would get worried.

I need to change back. Focussing hard, Seren thought about happy things. Just as her mum reached the door she expanded to her normal size and lay on the floor gasping.

"Are you all right, Seren?" Mum said as she

came into the room. "That was school on the phone. They said you'd been sick."

Seren looked up at her mum and wondered whether to tell her the truth. She didn't like lying, but Mum would go loopy if she knew Tilda had done magic.

"I'm fine," she said, trying to smile.

Mum looked at her for a long moment, then felt her forehead. "You seem okay. It's probably something you ate."

"I had spinach and pumpkin omelette at Tilda's last night," Seren said.

"Well, that would do it!" Mum laughed. "Your aunt has a creative approach to cooking."

"I think I left a book there, can I pop over and get it?" Seren asked.

"I can fetch it at lunchtime tomorrow, if you like?" Mum said.

"No! No, it's fine, I'd like to tell Aunt Tilda about National Children's Fiction Day."

"Not tonight," Mum said firmly. "Maybe after

school tomorrow. Just be home for tea this time."

Seren nodded and gave her mum a hug. "Thanks, Mum, you're the best."

"Now get some rest," Mum said, and left the room.

At school the next morning, Seren looked around for Freia. She hadn't been on the school bus and it wasn't a breakfast club day. Her friend still hadn't arrived by the time class started.

"No Freia," Miss Joy said, as she called out the names. "Her mum says she's not well."

Seren's tummy wobbled. Break time was hard enough with Freia to support her. If she was by herself, Billy would show no mercy.

As if sensing her thoughts, Billy sniggered and whispered to his friend Tim in the next seat.

"Do you have something to share with the class?" Miss Joy asked. Billy shook his head, but his grin was vicious.

When the bell rang for break, Seren headed

straight for the quiet garden. If she could sit in a corner unnoticed, Billy might find someone else to pick on.

Her plan worked. It was boring sitting by herself, but it was the nicest break time she'd had in ages.

She followed the same plan after lunch, hiding at the end of the willow walk, out of sight of the playground.

It was almost time to go in for afternoon class when Seren saw one of the playground assistants tidying away the equipment into the shed.

"I'll help with that, Mrs Clements," Seren said. That way Billy couldn't do anything to her on the way back to the classroom.

"Thank you, Seren, that's very kind. If you could gather up the skipping ropes and pop them in the shed, I'll go and check for stray tennis balls."

Seren nodded and gathered up the multi-coloured ropes. As she put them in a box on the shelf, she heard the shed door slam shut behind her.

"Mrs Clements, I'm still in here!" she called. There was no answer. Then she heard the sound of the padlock being threaded through and clicked into place.

She was stuck.

Chapter Nine

Seren pressed her nose up against the tiny window, but she couldn't see through the dirt. Footsteps approached the shed. The door rattled, followed by the sound of someone walking away. Seren guessed it was the playground assistant, making sure the shed was locked.

"Come back!" Seren yelled, "Let me out!"

But Mrs Clements didn't hear her. At that moment the bell rang and her cries were drowned out as all the children made their way chattering into school.

Seren clambered down and shook the door but it wouldn't budge. She gave it a kick before turning her shoulders against it. Dropping her head into her hands she began to cry.

A sound at the window made her look up. Someone was watching her through the glass and grinning. Billy!

I might have known, she thought. "Billy! Unlock the door. This isn't funny, I'm going to be late for Literacy. Miss Joy will take my golden time away!"

Billy just waved and dropped out of sight.

Seren looked round in a panic. What if no one found her? What if she was locked in all night? The equipment wasn't used at afternoon break and it seemed no one could hear her shouting.

"Come on, Seren, don't let Billy beat you," she said out loud. Pushing away from the door, Seren looked all around the shed. The window slid open, but it was far too small for her to get through.

As a person, maybe, she thought suddenly. But not as a cat. But how to turn into a cat without getting angry? Could she do it?

And then she remembered Billy's smirking face as he laughed through the window. She focussed on the nasty gleam in his eye, and on how much trouble she was in. As she pictured it, she became more and more angry. Her face grew hot and her skin tingled. The marching ants stomped across her skin and fur sprouted like new grass. In no time she was crouched on the floor, ready to spring for the window. Only she had forgotten to open it!

I can't open it with paws, Seren yowled in frustration. With a huge effort she forced herself to be calm – to change back into her human form. Once she was big she slid open the window as far as it would go. It was only a tiny space, was it big enough for even a cat to squeeze through?

I guess I'll find out, she thought. Then she shifted a box, to give her somewhere to jump from.

Well, here goes. She thought about Billy again, about the minutes ticking away. About Miss Joy calling the register and frowning when she didn't answer. Sure enough, the ants were back, her body shrank and her face itched as whiskers pinged from her cheeks.

Seren leapt onto the box and then jumped at the gap in the window. She missed the first time, bumping her nose on the glass. With a hiss of annoyance, she tried again and this time made it through.

After checking no one was watching she scampered round to the girls' toilets where she knew another window would be open.

It looked a long way up.

I'm never going to make it, Seren sighed. But if she didn't try, she wouldn't get back into school, and Billy would have won.

Seren crouched low to the ground. Then, with a huge leap, she soared upwards and caught hold of the open window. Scrabbling at the glass she discovered that claws didn't work on shiny surfaces. She pulled her claws in and used the pads of her feet to push against the glass. With a last enormous effort she scrambled over the window and landed safely on the floor.

So, cats do land on their feet. Seren laughed.

Her relief at getting into school made it easy to turn back into her human form. She flushed the toilet, ran her hands under the tap, and dashed to her classroom.

Miss Joy was just closing the register as she opened the door and peered round.

"Seren! Where have you been?" Miss Joy frowned. "It's not like you to be late back to class."

"I'm sorry, Miss Joy," Seren said as she slid into an empty seat. "I had to, er, go to the toilet. You know." She blushed.

"Okay," Miss Joy said, nodding in understanding as some of the class giggled. "Next time try to go at the beginning of break, please."

Seren let out a sigh of relief. Out of the corner of her eye she saw Billy pulling faces at her. Determined not to let him know how close it had been, she turned away and concentrated on her work. At least she was going to see Tilda after school. Then she could fix the spell and Seren could go back to being normal.

Chapter Ten

"This Billy sounds like a bad sort," Tilda said as Seren told her about all the cat-astrophes at school since Wednesday.

"He is," Seren agreed, "but I'm more worried about turning into a cat every time I get cross. What went wrong? Can you fix it?"

Tilda's face crumpled in a worried frown. "It's very odd," she said. "I've never known it to happen before."

"How many people have you turned into cats?"

"Well, you're the first. But I meant that spells don't generally leave lasting effects. Unless…"

"Unless what?" Seren asked, not sure she wanted to hear the answer.

"What day was it when we did the spell?" Tilda said distractedly.

"Tuesday."

"I mean what was the date?"

"Um." Seren thought. "The sixth of July?"

"Are you sure?" Tilda looked disappointed.

"Why don't you check your phone?" Seren suggested. She didn't see how the date mattered, but there was no point trying to get Aunt Tilda to drop something.

Tilda found her phone eventually, under a pile of old newspapers. "It's the 9th today," she said. "Which means the day before yesterday was the 7th! I knew it!"

Seren looked bewildered at her excitement. "And?"

"The 7th! The 7th day of the 7th month. And what time did I do the spell?"

"I'm not sure," Seren said, "But it was after tea. I remember because we had spinach and pumpkin omelettes." She pulled a face at the memory.

"So it might have been 7 o'clock?"

Seren shrugged.

"Don't you see? Seven is a powerful number in magic. 7 o'clock on the 7th day of the 7th month. It must have amplified the spell."

"Amplified?"

"Made it stronger."

"How do we fix it?" Seren wrapped a strand of black hair around her finger and nibbled the ends.

Aunt Tilda looked guilty. "I don't know if I can. It's strong magic. Stronger than mine."

"You mean I'm going to be stuck turning into a cat forever?" Seren wailed.

"I'm afraid you might be."

Seren sank into a chair and hugged her knees. Billy's bullying was looking like the least of her worries.

"Can *we* reverse the spell?" Seren heard someone say, as she huddled miserably in the armchair. She looked up, but Tilda was in the corner surrounded by books.

"I am not certain, Fizz," another voice said. "A triple-seven boosted spell might be too much for even our magic." The voice sounded reluctant to admit that such a thing was possible.

"Poor kitten. It distresses me to see her so sad."

Seren raised her head and spotted Fizz and Bang under the table. Had she imagined it, or did she understand them even when she wasn't a cat? Maybe she had transformed without realising it? She checked her arms quickly, but there was no white fur.

"Did you two say something?" she asked the cats, feeling a bit silly.

"You can understand us in your human form?" Fizz asked, looking up at Seren. "Most useful."

"How is that possible?" Seren frowned.

"Perhaps you are listening better," Bang suggested. "Speaking Cat is not so hard."

"Or it may be the spell," Fizz said. "Potent

stuff, triple-seven magic."

"So you said." Seren looked glum. "If you two don't know how to fix this I really am stuck."

"I am sorry you heard that. Do not give up," Fizz purred, jumping onto Seren's lap. "There will be something we can do."

"Yes," Bang said, leaping gracefully onto the back of the chair. "Once Matilda has gone to bed we will have a proper look."

Seren felt a tiny bit more hopeful.

"In the meantime, my dear, perhaps we can do something about that nasty Billy boy." Fizz rubbed her face against Seren's, drying her tears.

"Yes. We do not tolerate bullies. You leave him to us, my girl." Bang strutted to the end of the chair, stretched, and flexed his claws.

Seren gulped. "Don't hurt him," she said. "He's a pest, but hurting him would make me just as bad as him."

"We will not hurt him," Bang said. Something about the way he watched his claws made Seren doubt his words. But the huge tom cat frightened her a little, even when she was bigger than him.

"Okay," she said. "Having Billy leave me alone would certainly be nice."

"That is settled then." Bang leapt to the floor and began giving himself a wash.

Chapter Eleven

"Mum, I don't feel well,"

Seren tried to look poorly without overdoing it. Mum always saw through pretend tummy aches.

Mum came over and felt Seren's forehead. "You don't feel hot, but you do look a bit peaky."

"Can I stay home? Freia can tell me anything I've missed," Seren added. "And I promise I'll be quiet and won't bother you."

"Hmmm."

Seren waited. Mum didn't believe in time off school unless she or Bryn were really ill.

"If you have to work I can go to Aunt Tilda's," Seren added.

Mum looked at her suspiciously and Seren held her breath. Mentioning Aunt Tilda had been a mistake.

"You've been there a lot this week. You two aren't cooking something up together are you?" Mum tilted her head. "She didn't do anything *special*?"

Seren shook her head, hoping she didn't look as guilty as she felt.

"Well, I don't have any meetings today, so you won't have to go to your aunt's. As long as you promise to be quiet and rest I guess you can stay home."

Seren suppressed a relieved grin. Today was Friday. If she didn't go to school today that meant she and Tilda had three days to come up with a fix for her cat-astrophe before she had to face Billy again. That should be long enough, surely.

Seren was curled up on the sofa reading a book when she heard a scratch at the window. It was Fizz. Seren looked around to check Mum was nowhere in sight, before opening the window.

"Fizz! What are you doing here? You can't stay. Dad's allergic to cats. If you shed hair he'll know – he'll start sneezing."

"Matilda sent me. Your mother called to ask her what happened this week. She said you were sick. Matilda wanted to reassure herself that you were all right."

Seren hung her head, her cheeks flushing red. "I didn't mean for Tilda to worry. I just couldn't face going to school. Yesterday was awful!"

Fizz purred and rubbed her head against Seren's cheek. "You poor kitten. Bang and I are working on a plan."

"To fix the spell or frighten Billy?" Seren asked.

"A bit of both," Fizz admitted. "Do not let it concern you. Sit tight and leave it to us."

Seren nodded and shut the window as Fizz bounded away. For some reason the cat's words didn't make her feel better at all.

Chapter Twelve

"Hello, Mrs Adessi, is Seren in?"

Seren heard Freia at the door. She ran down the stairs then stopped when she saw Mum looking strangely at her.

"I thought you were poorly?" Mum said.

"I'm feeling much better now. A day resting and reading was just what I needed."

Mum didn't look convinced.

"I've brought Seren's homework," Freia said. Seren gave her a grateful smile for distracting Mum.

"You can come in for ten minutes," Mum said to Freia. "And then Seren needs to go back to bed."

The two girls went to Seren's room and shut the door.

"How was school?" Seren asked.

"Lonely without you." Freia pulled a face. "Billy was awful. He said you'd caught the lurgy in the boys' toilets and wouldn't be back at school for weeks."

"What is *with* him?" Seren stormed. "It makes me so cross."

"Don't get angry!" Freia said urgently, holding her hand up in warning. But it was too late. Seren's nose twitched and her face itched and suddenly Freia was the size of a giant.

"Oh, Seren!" Freia cried. She reached out a hand. "Can I stroke you? You're such a cute cat."

Seren purred and jumped onto Freia's lap. Suddenly the bedroom door opened and Mum stuck her head in.

"It's time for you to go, Freia. Seren needs to rest." She saw the cat and looked around the room. "Where is Seren? And where did that cat come from? You know we can't have cats in the house. Seren's dad is allergic."

She grabbed hold of Seren and carried her downstairs. Freia ran after them.

"I'm sorry, Mrs Adessi, I let the cat in. She was so sweet. I forgot about the allergy. Don't be cross with Seren. She said she felt sick, so she's in the bathroom."

"Seren!" Mum called up the stairs. "Freia is leaving. I'll come and check on you in a minute."

She opened the door and put the white cat down on the pavement. "Go on, cat, shoo!" she said.

Freia hovered in the doorway. Seren looked up at her and miaowed.

"Here is Seren's homework," Freia said, pulling a sheet of paper from her bag. "Tell her I hope she feels better soon."

Freia picked up the cat and hurried out of sight round the corner. As soon as she heard the front door close behind them she stopped.

"Seren, are you okay?" she whispered. The cat nodded.

"How are you going to get back in?"

Seren looked up at the house. Her bedroom window was open a fraction, but how was she going to reach it and get into the bathroom before Mum got there.

Freia followed her gaze. "If you climbed that tree you might be able to jump to the window. I can go and ring the doorbell and run away, that might buy you a few minutes."

Seren nuzzled Freia's face then leapt from her arms. As she clambered up the tree, she saw Freia dash back to the front door.

She was measuring the distance to her bedroom window when she heard the bell go. She had only moments to get in, change and lock herself in the bathroom. It was going to be close.

There was no time to think, or worry about the huge drop down to the ground if she missed. Seren bunched herself up and leapt. She misjudged the distance and slammed into the window.

Ouch. It's lucky cats have nine lives, she

winced, as she snuck through the gap. The thought made her giggle and she was still smiling as she turned back into her own form.

She was just closing the bathroom door when she heard Mum climbing the stairs.

"Nuisance kids," Mum said. "Ringing the bell and running away." She knocked on the door. "Are you feeling all right, Seren? Have you been sick?"

Seren felt terrible for lying to her mum, but she didn't know what else to do. Would Mum even believe that she was the cat?

"I feel a bit wobbly, Mum," Well that was true. "I think I'll go and lie down."

Please find a solution, Fizz, she thought as she went back to her room. Before Mum finds out her daughter's part cat.

Chapter Thirteen

It was only one week to the end of term. Seren couldn't wait. She'd survived the whole weekend and Monday and Tuesday without turning into a cat again.

Maybe the spell has worn off, she thought hopefully.

So far there had been no sight of Fizz and Bang teaching Billy a lesson. Seren wasn't sure if she was disappointed or relieved. Billy was being as horrible as ever.

On Monday he'd taken all the books from her drawer and hidden them. Miss Joy had been nice about it, but Seren had been embarrassed at having to work on scrap paper. She'd felt tingly and had run off to the girls' toilets, but she hadn't sprouted fur.

Tuesday had been worse. Billy had taken her clothes during PE and dropped them in a puddle on the changing room floor. A suspiciously smelly puddle. Seren had been forced to stay in her PE kit until home time, because there wasn't enough lost property to get changed into.

If I survived both of those times without becoming a cat, I think the spell must have gone. Seren grimaced. Fingers crossed!

The playground was crowded by the time Seren and Freia got out at morning break. They'd offered to stay and help Miss Joy clean the whiteboard.

Billy's taunting started before they'd even decided what game to play.

"Teacher's pet, teacher's pet! Seren is a teacher's pet. What are you, her little pet cat?"

Seren gave Billy her best *I don't care* stare and dragged Freia over to the skipping ropes. Billy followed, miaowing and pretending to be a cat.

Just then two real cats jumped over the stone wall and landed in the playground. It was Fizz and Bang.

Oh no, thought Seren. Not now guys. She wanted to tell them to shoo, but was worried the teachers would realise she knew them.

"Aw, look at the cute kitties," Freia said. "Let's stroke them."

A crowd gathered around the cats, but Fizz and Bang took no heed. They looked like they were searching for something. Seren had a pretty good idea what.

"Hey, Billy, let's see if it's true that cats always land on their feet," Tim yelled. He stalked towards the cats with his hand out, saying, "Here, kitty, kitty, nice kitty."

Billy hung back, a wary look on his face. Fizz and Bang ignored Tim's outstretched hand and ran towards Billy. He yelped and turned away, shielding his face.

"Ugh, get them away from me. I *hate* cats."

Freia began to giggle and some of the other children joined in. Nadeem and Misaki and other children Billy had terrorised.

Seren smiled too. Maybe Fizz and Bang's idea wasn't so bad. It was nice to see Billy getting teased for a change.

Fizz wrapped herself around Billy's legs, tangling round and round until Billy fell backwards. As he landed in a heap on the floor, Bang jumped onto his tummy and hissed at him.

"Get them away from me!" Billy pleaded. He sounded terrified.

Seren went nearer and took in his pale face, glistening with sweat. Tears sparkled in his eyes as he stared wildly at Fizz and Bang.

"Guys," Seren said quietly, hoping Fizz and Bang would hear, "I think that's enough."

The cats turned to look at Seren. "But this boy is mean to you," Fizz mewed, swatting Billy with a paw.

"He calls you names and makes you cry," Bang

yowled, lifting a paw and flexing his claws.

At the sight of the claws, Billy moaned and his face crumpled. "Don't hurt me!"

"But if we frighten him and make him miserable, that means we're bullies too," Seren murmured. She went up to Fizz and Bang and gently shooed them away.

"Are you sure, Seren?" Fizz asked, as she walked off. Seren gave a tiny nod, not wanting anyone to see her talking to the cats.

Once the cats had jumped back over the wall, Seren ran to Billy and held out her hand. "Are you all right?" she asked.

Billy glared at her. His face was blotchy and wet. Then he realised people were still laughing, and he let Seren pull him to his feet.

"Thank you," he muttered, not meeting her eyes.

Seren smiled. "You're welcome."

"Why did you help me?" he asked suddenly.

She gave a shrug. "No one should be

frightened, not even you."

Billy's face reddened. "I'm sorry I've been horrible."

"Why were you? What did I ever do to you?"

"You're always going on about cats like they're so amazing!" He blurted out. "I hate cats."

"And that means you hate me? That doesn't make sense." Seren put her hands on her hips.

"Anyway if I'm mean first then other people can't be nasty to me," Billy added. He looked like he wanted to say more, but Miss Joy was heading over to see what all the fuss was about.

"Don't tell anyone I'm scared of cats, okay?" he said.

Seren thought half the playground probably knew by now, but she just nodded.

"Okay."

"Billy!" she called, as he ran off towards his friends. He stopped and glanced over his shoulder.

"Cats aren't so bad. If you want, I can help you."

He shook his head and turned away. But Seren thought she saw a glimmer of gratitude in his eyes.

Chapter Fourteen

For the first time in ages Seren was looking forward to break time. Since Fizz and Bang's visit the day before, Billy had stayed well away from the girls. In fact Seren hadn't seen him at all.

"What shall we play?" she asked Freia as they headed into the playground.

"How about hopscotch?" Freia suggested, pointing to where some of their friends were already playing.

Seren nodded and they headed over. As they passed the willow walk, Seren heard a noise like someone whimpering.

"I'll catch you up," she said to Freia, and dashed into the willow walk before Freia could ask questions.

At the far end, in the gloom where she often sat, was the very person she used to come here to avoid. Billy. And he was crying.

"Billy?" Seren said gently.

"Go away!"

"What's wrong?" Seren asked in concern, perching on the bench next to him.

"Nothing," he said, wiping his nose with his sleeve.

"It doesn't look like nothing," Seren joked.

"Go ahead! Laugh. Why not, everyone else is."

"What do you mean?" Seren thought she knew, and she wanted to say *It serves you right*, or *Now you know how it feels*. But she kept quiet. The look of terror on Billy's face the day before was still in her mind. And what he'd said about being mean first to stop others hurting him.

"Someone told my brothers about the cats. They thought it was right funny. Locked me in all night. And now Tim and Freddie won't quit. They keep miaowing at me and laughing their heads off."

"Locked you in where?" Seren asked, ignoring the bit about Tim and Freddie. They'd laughed at her plenty of times when Billy had done something cruel.

"My brothers think it's funny to lock me in the laundry with my step-mum's cats. Nasty brutes."

"Your brothers?"

"The cats. They scratch and bite and hiss at me. Mum locks me in there when I'm naughty, but usually only for an hour or two. But my brothers shut me in all night."

He hiccupped back a sob.

Seren reached over and touched his hand but Billy snatched it away. "Why don't you tell someone?" Seren said.

"What's the point?" Billy hissed. "If Dad doesn't care, who else will?"

Seren didn't know what to say. Poor Billy. No wonder he was nasty if his own family were mean to him.

"Tell Miss Joy. She's brilliant," Seren urged.

"And I can help you with the cat thing, if you like?"

She wondered whether to turn into a cat, but guessed that might be a really bad idea. "I can introduce you to my Aunt's cats, Fizz and Bang," she suggested instead. "They're lovely."

Billy shook his head.

Just then a voice called from the end of the willow walk. "Seren, are you in there?"

"It's Freia," Seren said, jumping to her feet. "I'd better go."

Billy stared silently at the floor.

"Talk to Miss Joy," Seren said again, then ran to join Freia in the sunshine.

Chapter Fifteen

It was Saturday morning and Seren was doing her homework in her room. She heard the phone ringing in the lounge but she ignored it. Freia was at ballet and no one else ever called her.

"Seren!" Mum yelled up the stairs a few moments later. "It's Aunt Tilda. She wants to speak to you." Mum sounded suspicious. "What are you two up to now?"

"Nothing," Seren said as she ran down the stairs. Why did Aunt Tilda want to talk to her?

"Hi, Aunt Tilda," Seren said as she took the handset from her mum, "Mum said you wanted to talk to me?"

"Is she listening?" Aunt Tilda murmured.

Seren looked around carefully, but Mum had

left the room. "No."

"Good. I think I have a solution to your cat problem." Tilda hesitated. "It's really strange. There was a book I'd never seen before on my desk this morning and it was open at exactly the page I needed. I don't know how it got there."

Seren had a pretty good idea, but she kept quiet. If Fizz and Bang wanted their identity – and help – to remain a secret, it wasn't for her to give them away.

"It won't stop you turning into a cat, but it will let you control it. There's a spell for changing and a spell for changing back."

Seren's heart sank. "So I still might turn into a cat if I get angry?"

"It's possible," Tilda said. "But you just have to say the spell quickly and you should change back. With practice I think you'll be fine."

"What are the spells?" Seren asked. "Are they hard?"

"They're not, but I think you should come

here. You don't want to practice at home where your mum might see."

Seren thought about Friday night, and her mum dumping her on the doorstep. "Definitely not," she agreed. "Let me ask Mum."

She put her hand over the handset and yelled, "Mum? Can I go to Aunt Tilda's for lunch? She promises it's just pasta."

Mum came in the room drying her hands on a tea towel. "Tilda's again? You two have been thick as thieves these last two weeks. I don't know. What with Bryn always at his friends' houses, I'm beginning to wonder if I even have children."

"You're always saying you'd like some peace and quiet." Seren beamed.

Mum laughed. "Fair enough. You can go, but make sure Tilda sends you home by seven."

Seren nodded. She didn't want to do spells at 7 o'clock again.

"Are you sure the spells aren't hard?" Seren asked,

after she and her aunt had enjoyed a glass of milk with a slice of sweet potato and blueberry pie.

"The words of the spell don't matter, as long as you remember them," Tilda said as she cleared the plates. "When you say them the first time, I have to wave my wand like this." She picked it up from the table.

"Wait!" Seren said. "Let's agree the words first."

"How about something like, 'Fancy this, fancy that. Turn this girl into a cat'?'" Tilda suggested.

Seren nodded. "And what about, 'Give a hiss, give a purr. Give me skin instead of fur'? To turn me back?"

"Yes, I like it."

"Let's write them down," Seren said quickly. "I don't want to get it wrong."

They wrote the spells down carefully and Seren practised saying them until she got them the same every time.

"Right. Now for the magic bit."

They went into the study and Aunt Tilda fetched a small spell book with thick yellow pages. Seren wondered where Fizz and Bang had found it.

"You say the words and I'll wave the wand," Tilda said. "Then the words should work any time you need them, without me and the wand."

Seren swallowed and her stomach felt full of buzzing flies. Something brushed her leg and looked down to see Fizz and Bang at her feet. Their presence made her feel better. They would make sure nothing went wrong.

With a deep breath Seren repeated the first spell, "Fancy this, fancy that. Turn this girl into a cat."

She watched as Tilda made a complicated set of movements with her wand. This time the transformation happened super-fast. One minute she was standing watching her aunt, and the next she was between Fizz and Bang on the floor.

"I've thought of a problem," Seren said. It sounded like "Miaow, miaow, mew mew." Aunt

Tilda looked at her with her head tilted.

"Sorry, Seren, I can't understand you. Did you say the spell?"

Seren shook her head. She turned to Fizz. "Will the spell work if I say it in Cat? And how do I let Aunt Tilda know when I'm saying it."

Fizz waved her tail in concern. "That did not occur to us. Oh dear."

Seren's own tail twitched. "Nothing ever goes right!"

"Do not fret," Fizz said, coming to nuzzle her. "Can you change back without the spell? You have managed it before."

"I can try," Seren miaowed.

"Good girl."

Seren concentrated on happy thoughts, and found herself springing back into her human form.

"Oh thank goodness," Tilda said. "I can't understand you when you're a cat. I didn't know when you were saying the words. Do you need the second spell? You changed back by yourself."

"I'd rather have it just in case. How about I tap my paw three times and we do the spell on three?"

Tilda nodded. Seren said the rhyme again, "Fancy this, fancy that. Turn this girl into a cat."

Once she had transformed she looked up at Tilda. Her aunt loomed over her like a giant. Seren tapped her paw three times and miaowed, "Give a hiss, give a purr. Give me skin instead of fur."

Aunt Tilda waved her wand in a complex pattern and Seren was a girl again.

"Hurrah," they both said. "It worked!"

"So I can be a cat whenever I want?" Seren asked. For the first time it didn't seem awful. "Actually that could be fun." And then she thought of something, and her face fell.

"I guess it's time I told Mum."

Chapter Sixteen

Seren bounced happily onto the school bus on Monday morning. She no longer had to worry about turning into a cat by accident. If she did, she just had to recite the spell, and she would change back. Billy didn't scare her any more either, not now she knew his secret.

It had been hard telling Mum about the spell. She hadn't wanted to, but she didn't like lying to Mum either. In the end she'd just said that Tilda had turned her into a cat once. No reason for her to worry that her daughter might be out roaming the rooftops.

And now she had another reason to look forward to the summer holidays. If she got bored she could jump out the window and climb down the tree in search of adventure.

What did cats do all day? She decided to ask Fizz and Bang next time she saw them.

Freia was in breakfast club, so Seren walked into school alone, smiling in the morning sunshine. Three more days of school and it would be the end of term.

She was imagining all the cool things she could do in the holidays when she heard taunting shouts echoing round the playground. It sounded like Billy's friends, Tim and Freddie.

Seren's hands clenched in dread before her fear turned to anger. It was a sound she had heard too often from Billy – she wasn't going to let another person suffer as she had.

Determined to stop the boys bullying anyone else, Seren headed towards the raised voices. They were coming from behind the temporary classroom used by Year 6. Seren peered around the corner, ready to run for a teacher if it was something she couldn't handle.

There were only three boys in the shadows. She was right, two of them were Tim and Freddie, but the third was Billy. It seemed the boys were having an argument, not bullying another child.

Seren smiled in relief and began to retrace her steps. Then she heard crying.

"Just leave me alone," someone said. It sounded like Billy.

"Not so hard now, are you, Billy-boy?" Tim sneered. "My brother had a chat with one of your stepbrothers yesterday. He said you're a scaredy cat."

"Don't you mean scared *of* cats!" Freddie added.

"Poor little Billy, locked up by his wicked step-mother. You should be in a fairy tale." Tim laughed nastily. "Except you haven't got a fairy godmother to rescue you."

Yes he has, Seren thought fiercely. She recited the spell quickly under her breath and dropped her bag behind a bush as she felt herself transform.

She was only a small cat, but she had long claws and she was fast. Without stopping to wonder if it was a good idea, Seren bunched her muscles and bounded round the corner.

Tim and Freddie had shoved Billy up against the classroom wall. They were much bigger than Billy. Seren had never noticed before. Billy was their leader. But now he looked like a frightened little mouse being tormented by feral cats.

With a yowl that echoed eerily in the shadows, Seren leapt at Tim and landed on his head. She flexed her claws, not deep enough to make Tim bleed, but enough to hurt a little bit.

"Ow! Gerroff me, stupid cat."

Seren sensed Billy quail at the word cat, and heard Freddie roar with laughter. Seren sprang from Tim and landed on Freddie's shoulder. She hissed loudly in his ear and batted him across the face with her claws shielded. She only wanted to stop the boys hurting Billy, not injure them.

Her plan worked. In the darkness they didn't

realise it was only one little white cat that had pounced, and in their minds they remembered the two fierce cats who had jumped on Billy.

"Come on, let's go," Freddie yelled. Tim nodded and the two boys ran off back to the playground.

Seren dropped down next to Billy, where he had slumped on the floor with his hands over his head. Gently she rubbed her head against his knee and purred. But she couldn't risk giving herself away, so she bounded off and hid in the willow walk while she miaowed the transformation spell.

Once she was herself again, Seren grabbed her bag and went to find Billy. He was still behind the classroom, his arms wrapped around his shoulders.

"Hey, Billy. I heard Tim and Freddie being mean. Are you all right?"

"Go away," Billy said, but without force.

"No." Seren hunkered down next to him. "I heard what they said. About your step-mum. Did you speak to Miss Joy?"

Billy shook his head.

"Come with me now. Please?" Seren didn't give him a chance to answer. She pulled him up by his arm and tugged him with her into school.

Miss Joy was in the classroom marking maths books. Seren knocked on the door.

"The bell hasn't gone yet, Seren," Miss Joy called as she raised her head to see who it was.

"Please, Miss, can we come in?" Seren called back.

Miss Joy looked puzzled and put down her paperwork. As she got closer to the door her eyes widened in surprise. Seren guessed she'd spotted Billy.

Their teacher pulled open the door and ushered them in. "What happened?" she asked in concern, looking at Billy's tear-streaked face.

"Tim and Freddie, Miss," Seren said. Then she glanced at Billy and hurried on before he could stop her. "But he's having trouble at home as well. His step-mum and step-brothers."

Miss Joy didn't look surprised and Seren wondered how much she already knew.

"Okay, Seren, thank you for bringing him to me. You can go now."

Seren hesitated. Before Miss Joy ordered her to leave, she said quickly to Billy, "The cat thing? Come to my Aunt's house one day. I'll help."

Billy looked like he wanted to say no. But he took a big gulp of air and then nodded.

Seren shone him a wide smile and left the room. Maybe Billy wasn't so bad after all.

As Seren walked to the bus with Freia after school that day, she saw Billy shuffling along with his hands deep in his pockets.

"Don't forget my offer, Billy," Seren called as they walked past. "I meant it, I'm happy to help."

Billy looked up and his face flushed deep red. He glanced around, as if to check no one was listening, and then he nodded.

"Great!" Seren felt Freia tug her arm. "I'll talk

to you tomorrow." Billy nodded again and ducked his head.

"So Billy is your friend now?" Freia asked, once they were far enough ahead of Billy to be out of earshot.

Seren looked at Freia in concern. Her best friend sounded odd. "Is that all right?"

"It's just a bit weird. He's been awful to you all year and suddenly you're happy to forgive him." Freia folded her arms and turned to glare at Seren.

"He said sorry," Seren shrugged. "And he has a really hard time at home. I think we should give him a chance."

Freia shook her head, sending her blonde plaits flying.

"Come on, Freia," Seren said, "Don't be mad at me. It's nearly the summer holidays. We can have loads of fun together! And won't it be nicer knowing Billy won't be mean when we come back next term?"

Freia chewed her lip. "I guess so." Then she

smiled. "What shall we do this weekend?" She hooked her arm through Seren's and pulled her towards the waiting bus.

Seren grinned. Billy might be all right, but Freia was her best friend in the world.

Printed in Great Britain
by Amazon.co.uk, Ltd.,
Marston Gate.